SILLY LILLY

AND THE FOUR SEASONS

Agnès Rosenstiehl

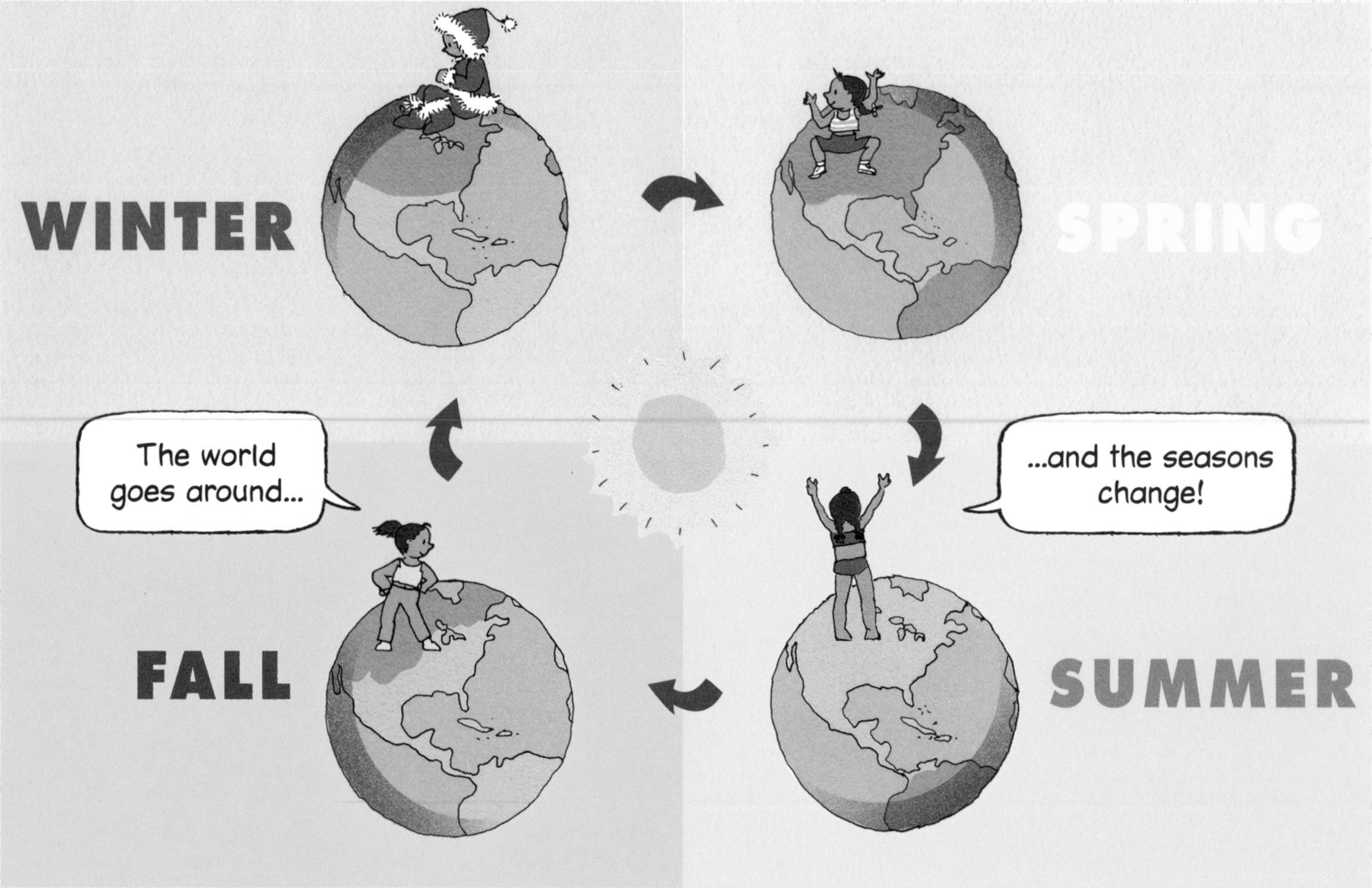
WINTER
SPRING
The world goes around...
...and the seasons change!
FALL
SUMMER

SILLY LILLY

AND THE FOUR SEASONS

A TOON BOOK BY
Agnès Rosenstiehl

TOON BOOKS IS AN IMPRINT OF CANDLEWICK PRESS

for Roro

Editorial Director: FRANÇOISE MOULY
Advisor: ART SPIEGELMAN

Book Design: FRANÇOISE MOULY & JONATHAN BENNETT

A TOON BOOK

 Printed in Singapore by Tien Wah Press (Pte.) Ltd. Library of Congress Control Number: 2007941869

ISBN 13: 978-0-9799238-1-4 ISBN 10: 0-9799238-1-6

11 12 13 14 15 16 TWP 10 9 8 7 6 5 4 3

www.TOON-BOOKS.com

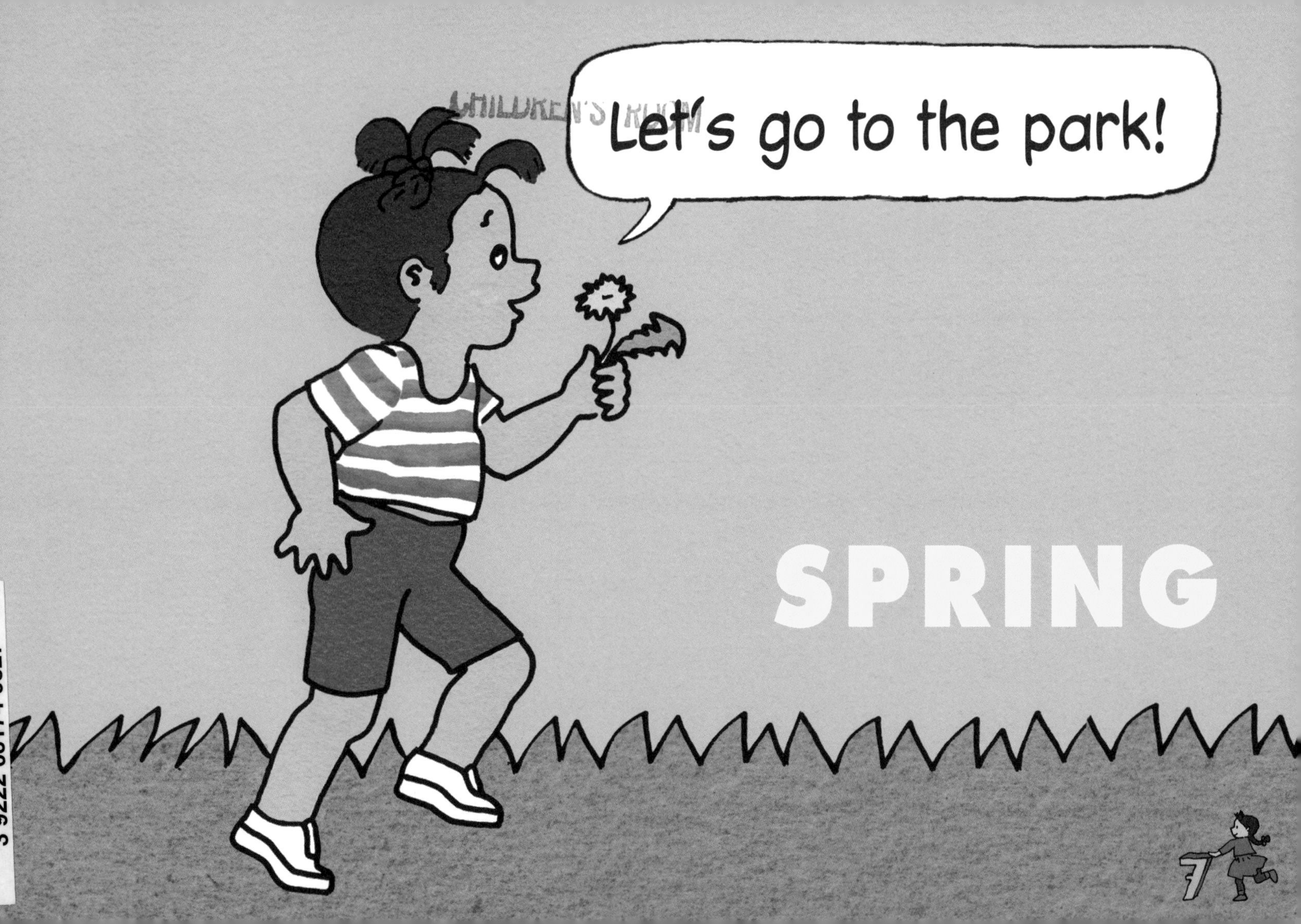
Let's go to the park!
SPRING

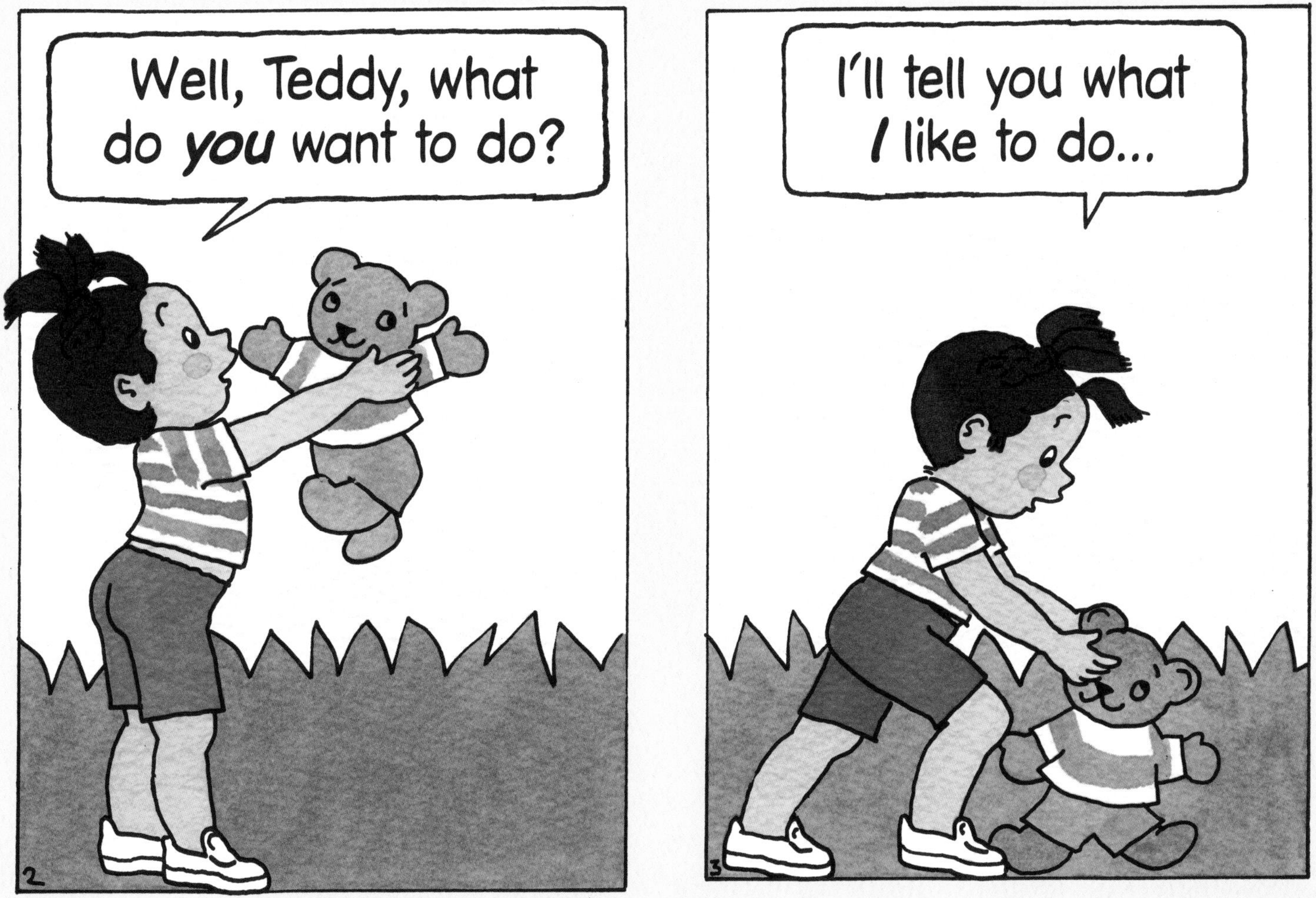
Well, Teddy, what do *you* want to do?
I'll tell you what *I* like to do...

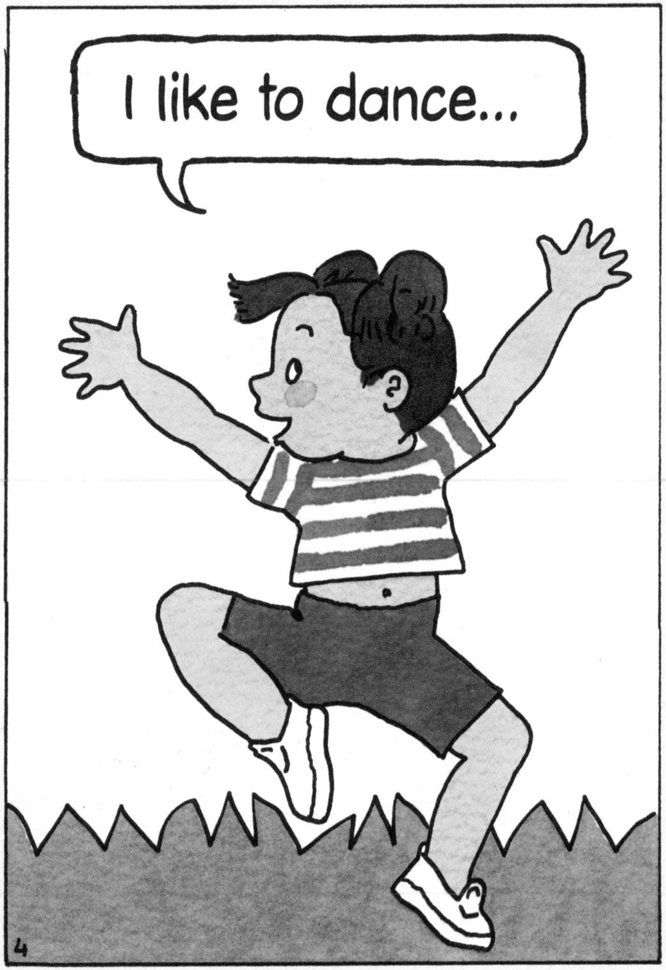
I like to dance...
4

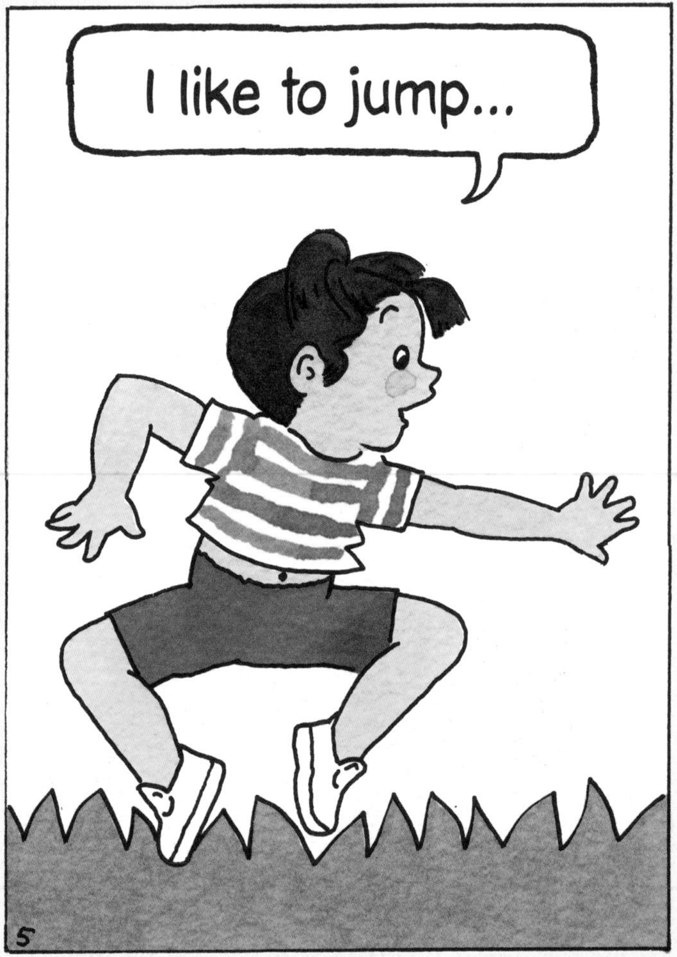
I like to jump...
5

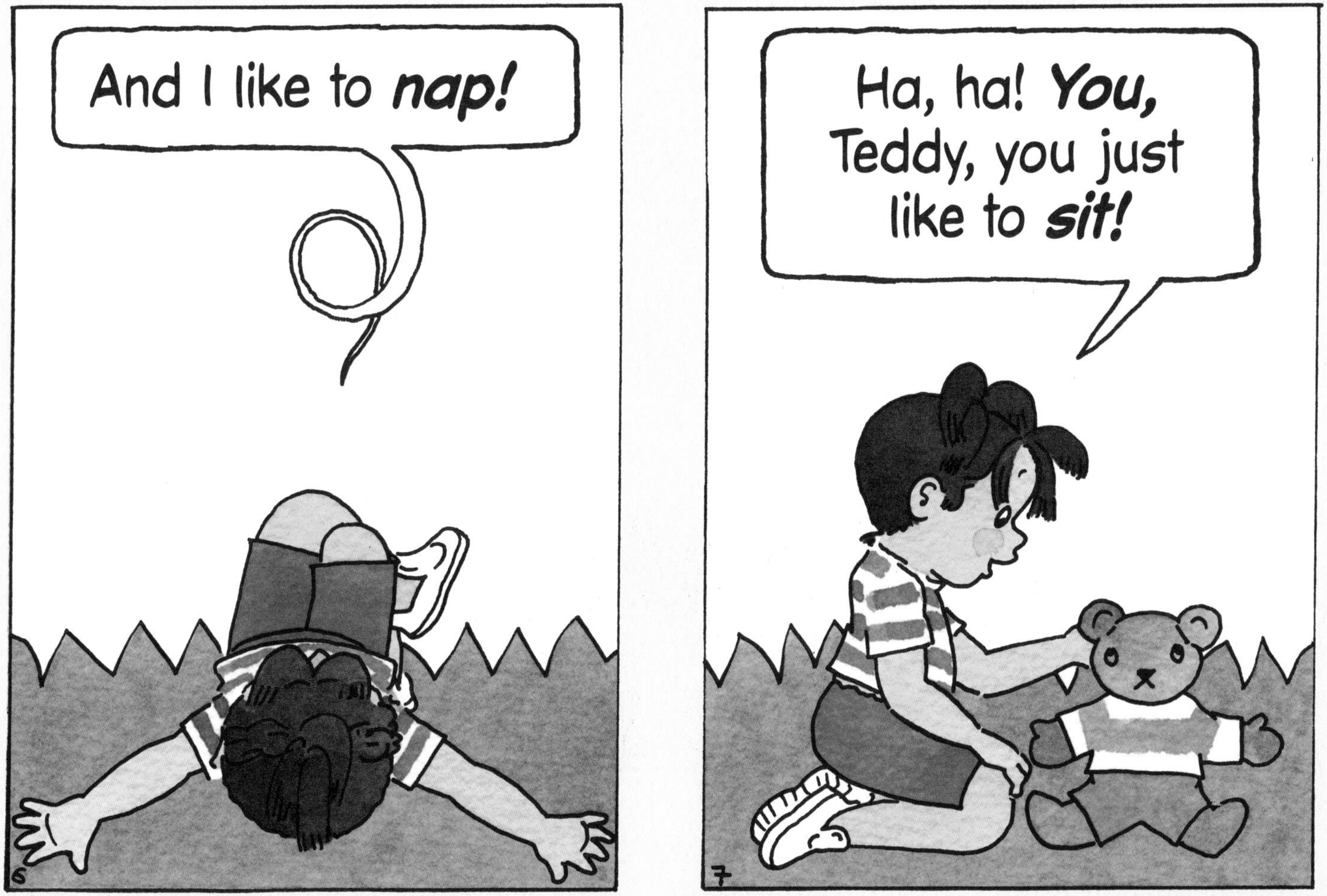
And I like to ***nap!***
Ha, ha! ***You,*** Teddy, you just like to ***sit!***

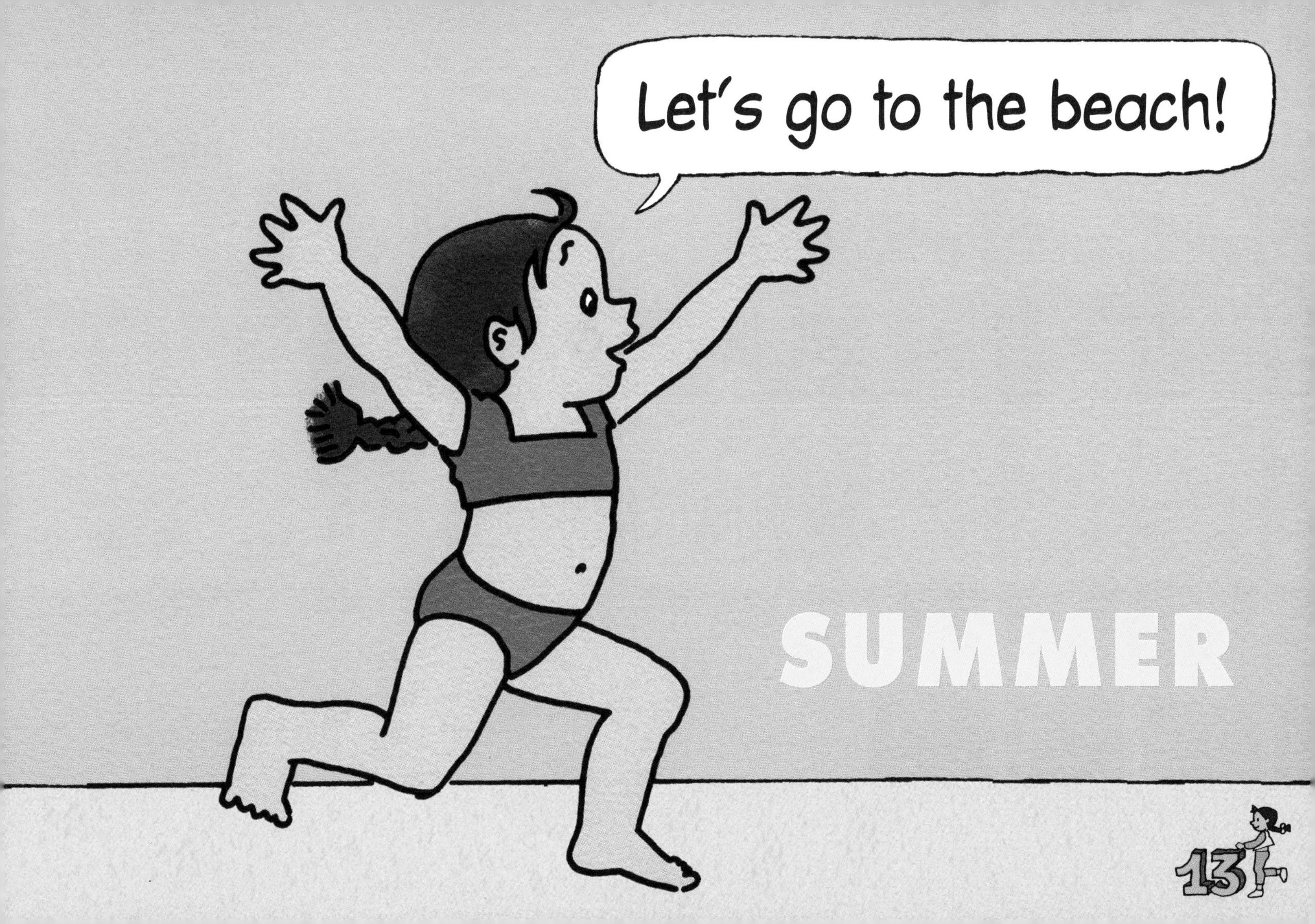
Let's go to the beach!
SUMMER

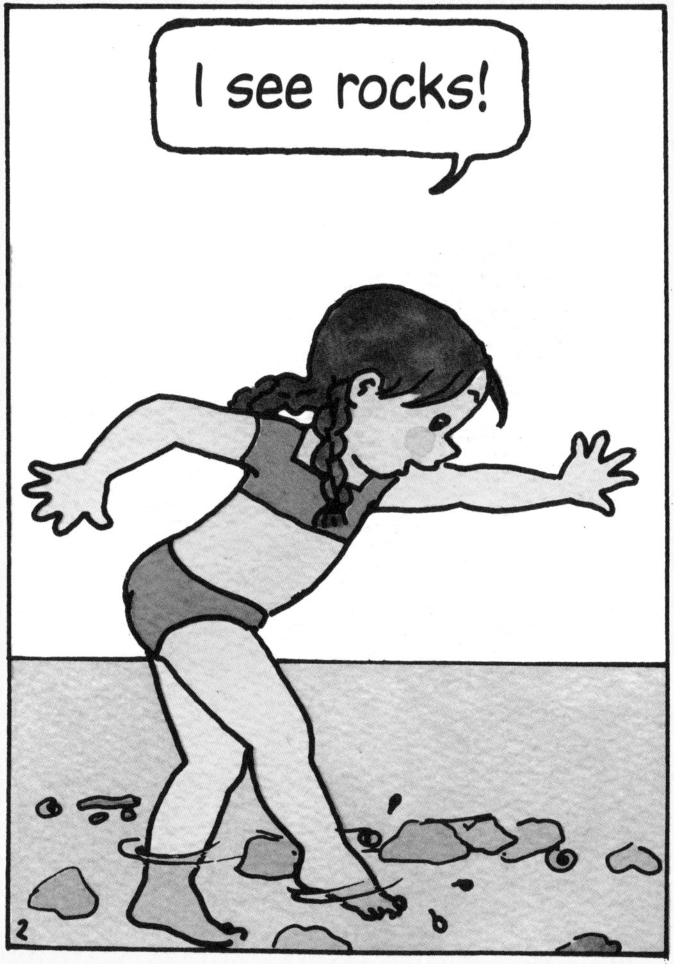
I see rocks!
2

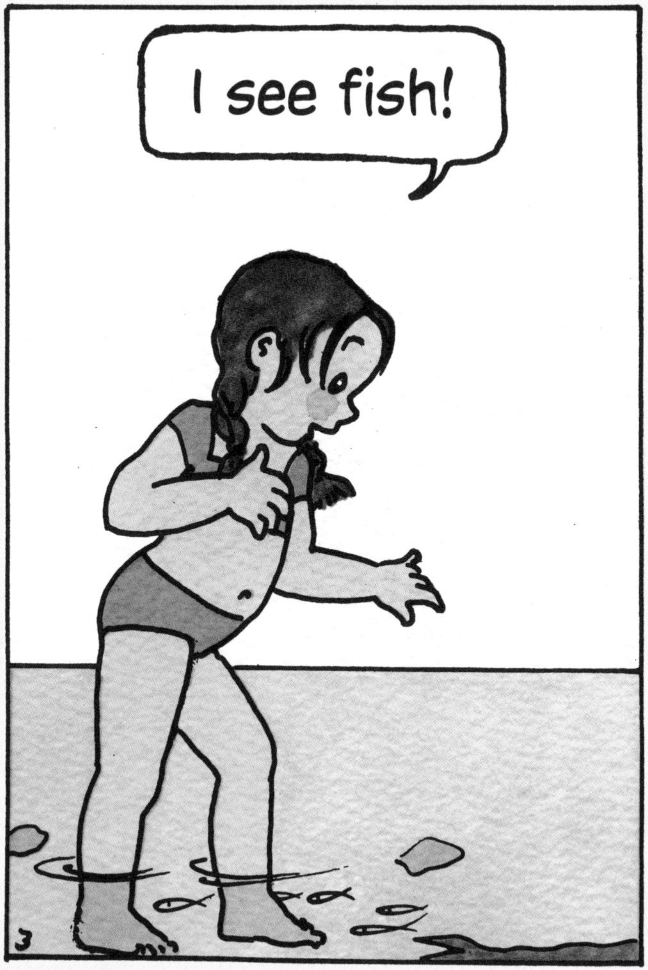
I see fish!
3

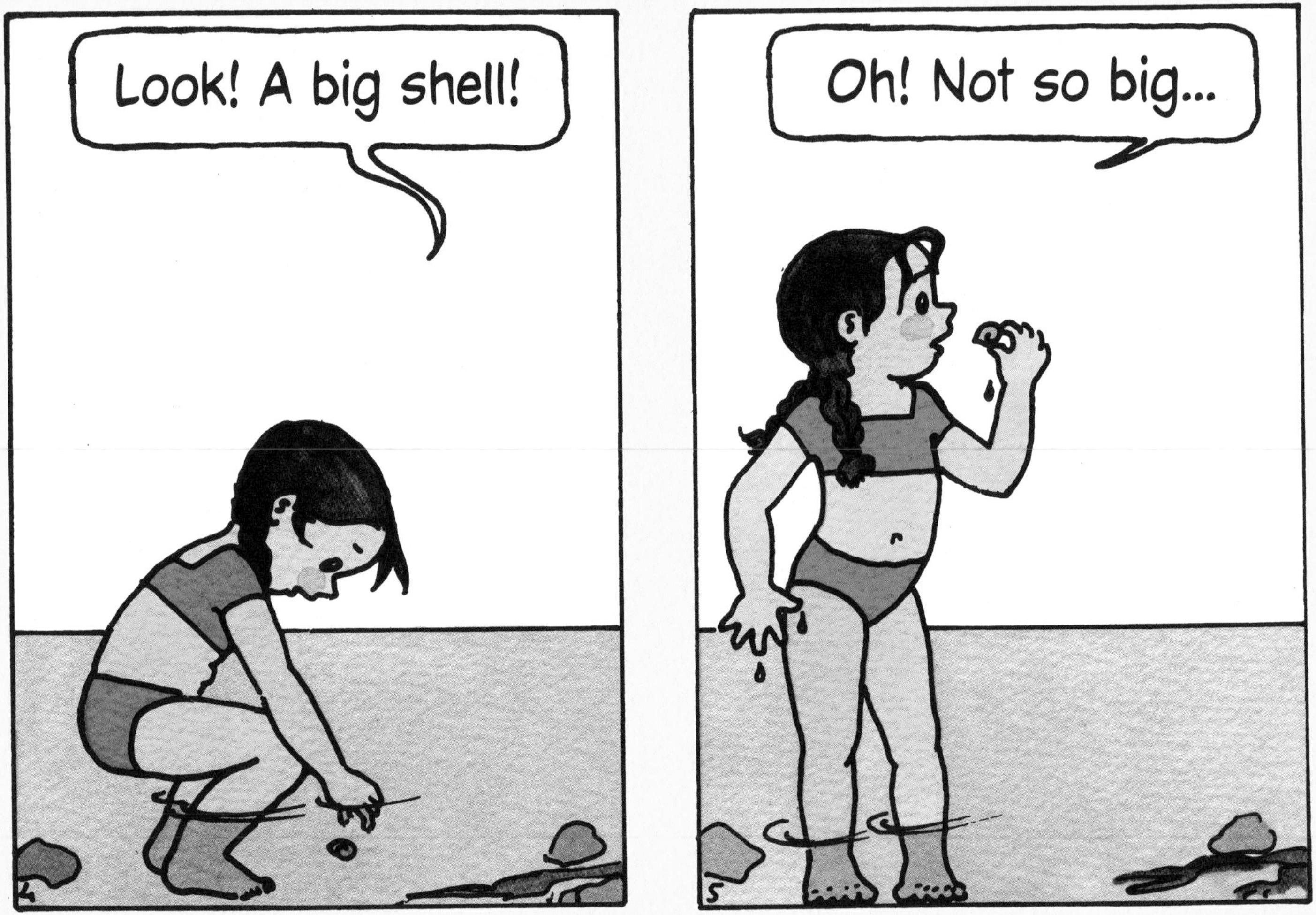
Look! A big shell!
Oh! Not so big...

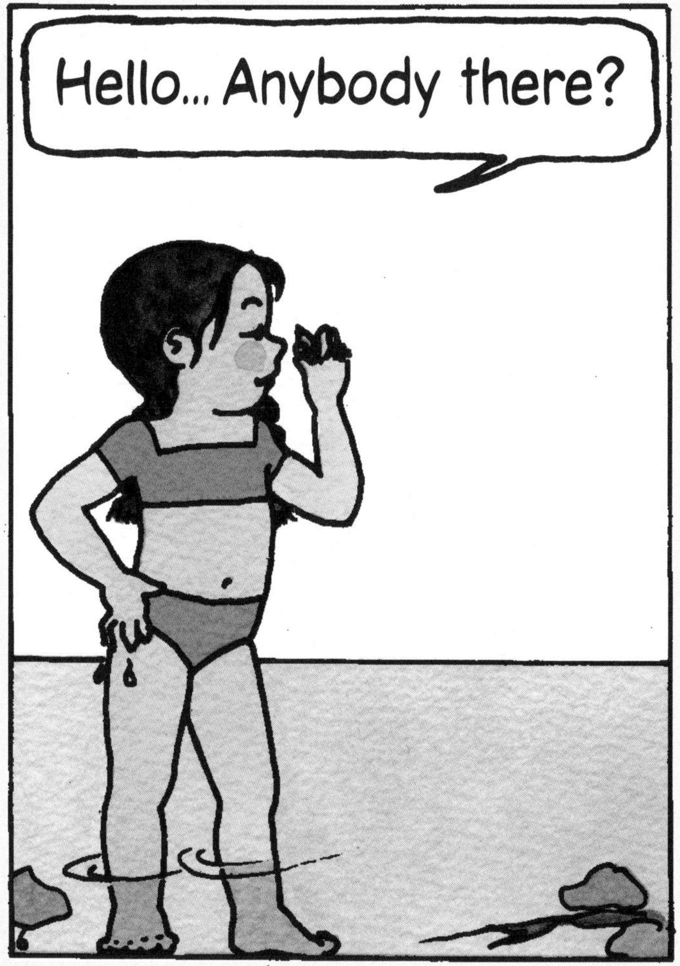
Hello... Anybody there?

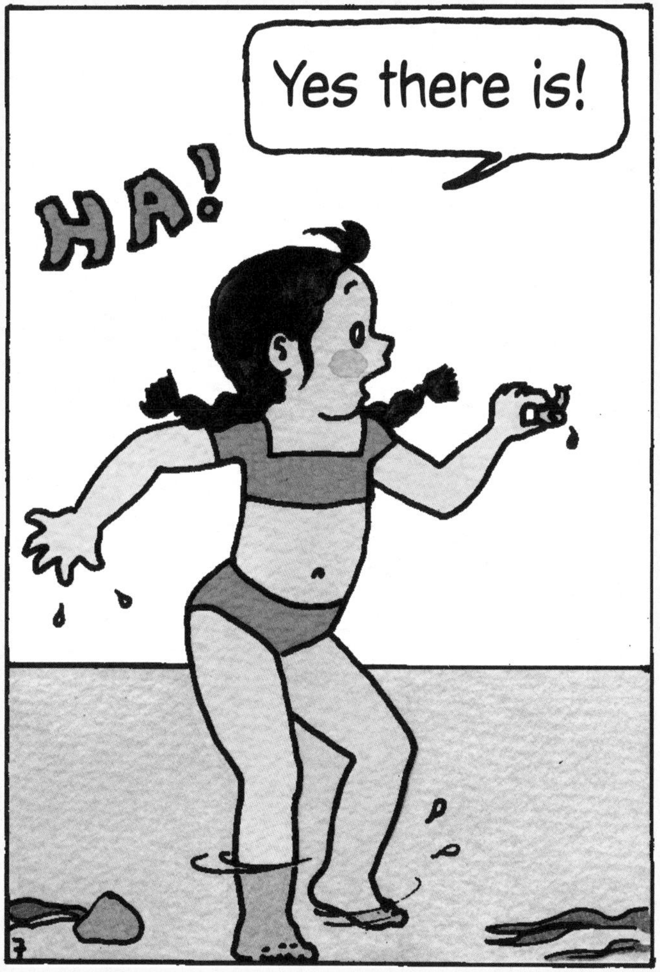
Yes there is!
HA!

18

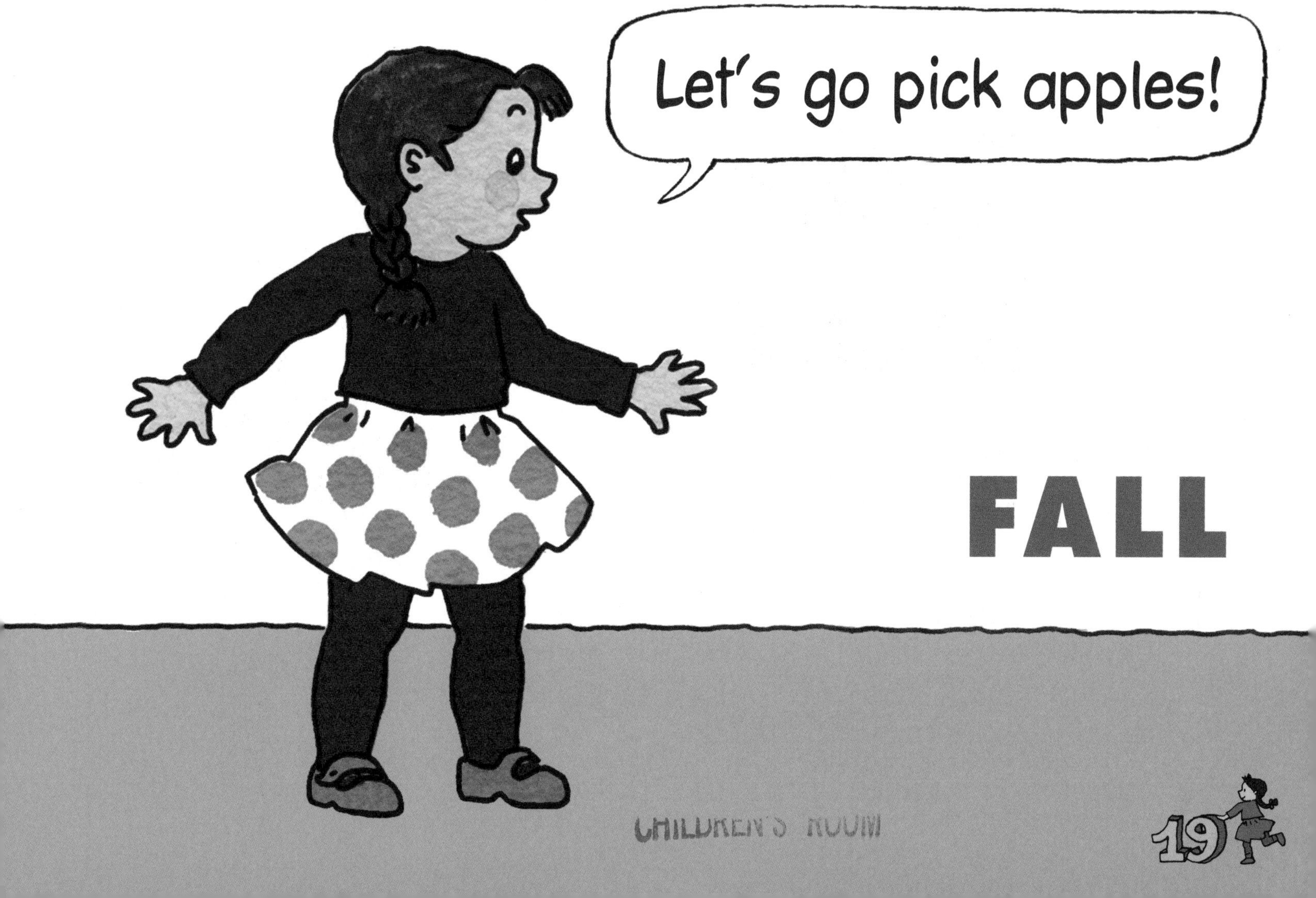
Let's go pick apples!

FALL

SILLY LILLY

AND THE APPLES

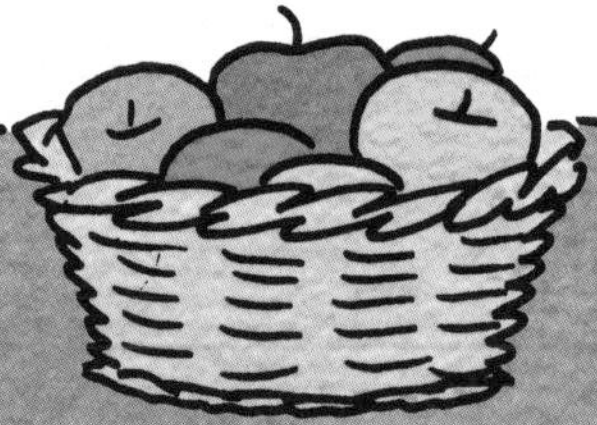

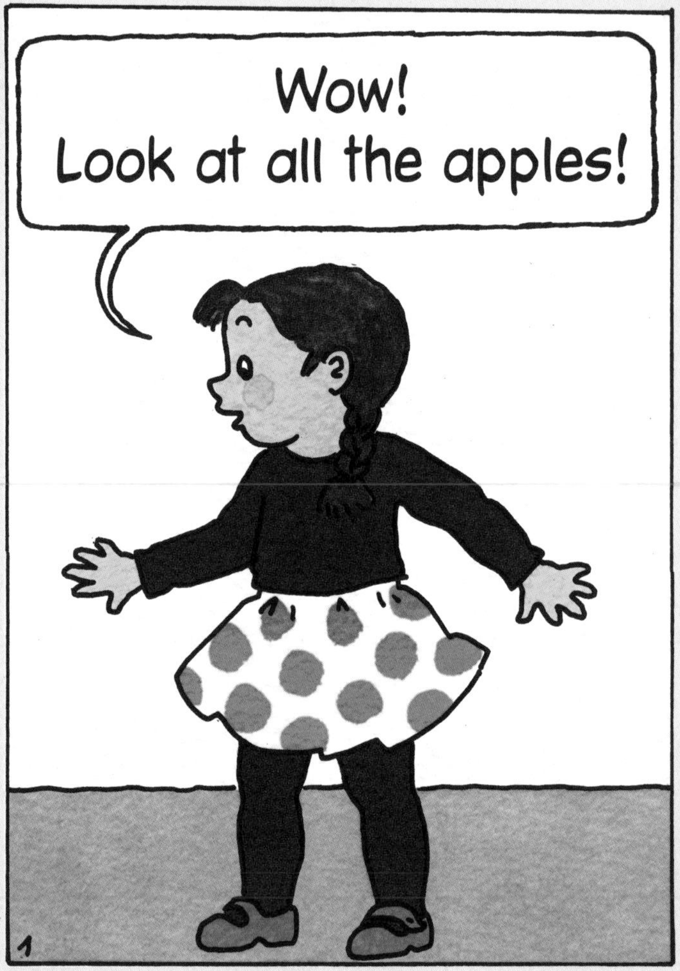
Wow!
Look at all the apples!
1

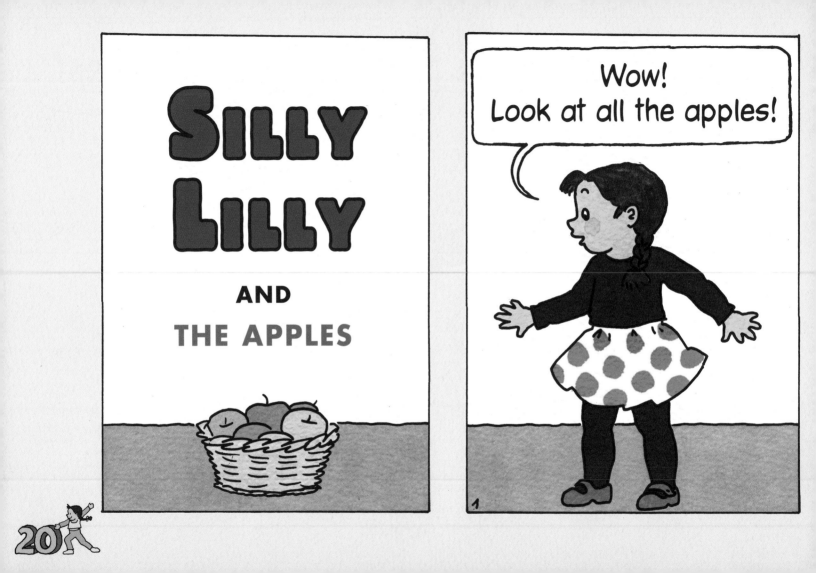

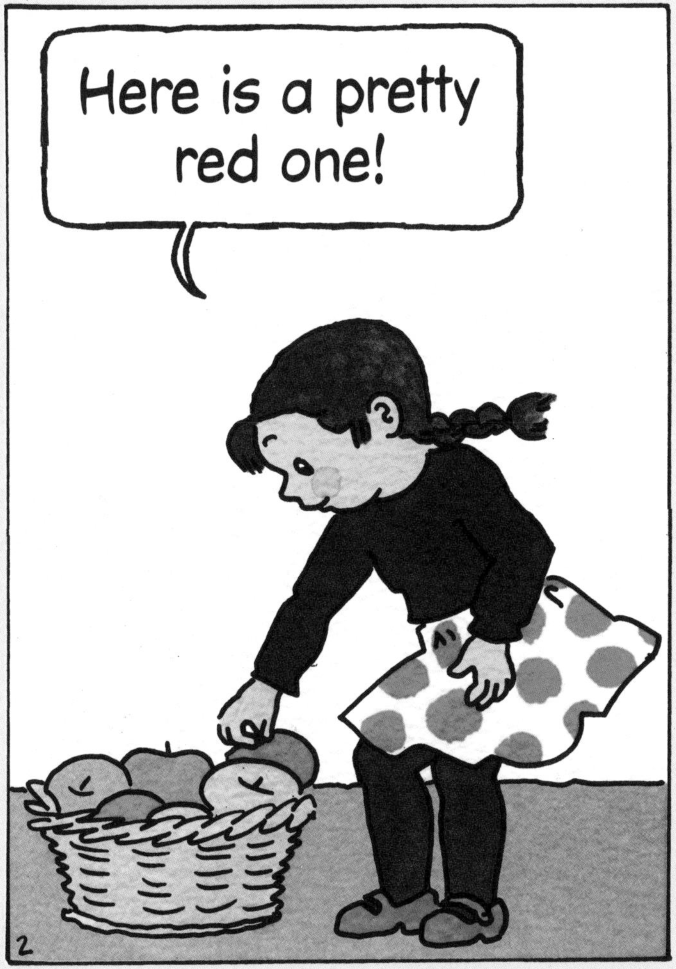
Here is a pretty red one!
2

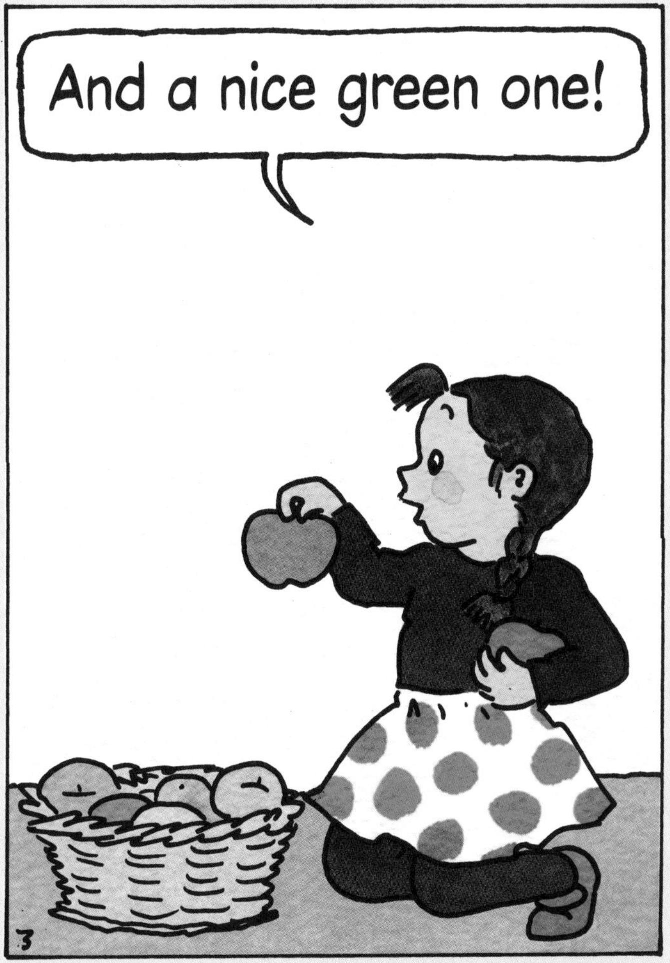
And a nice green one!
3

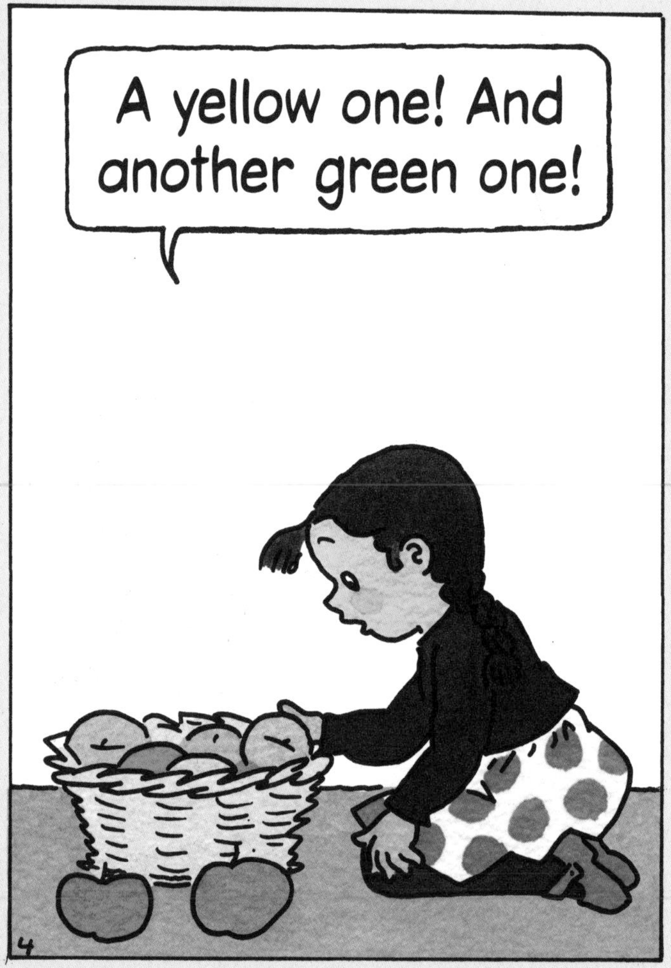
A yellow one! And another green one!

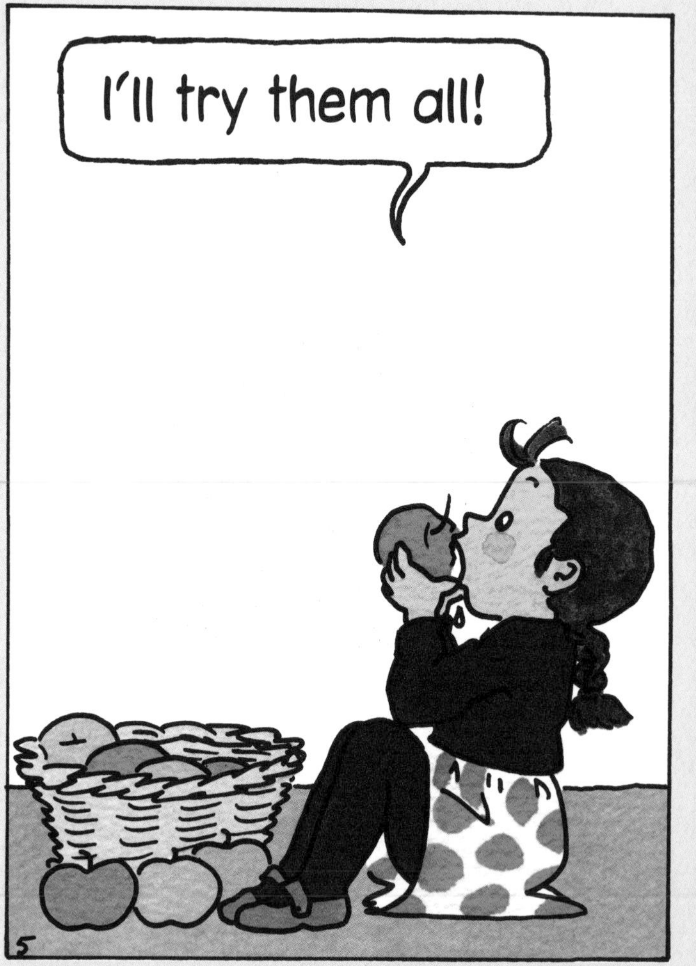
I'll try them all!

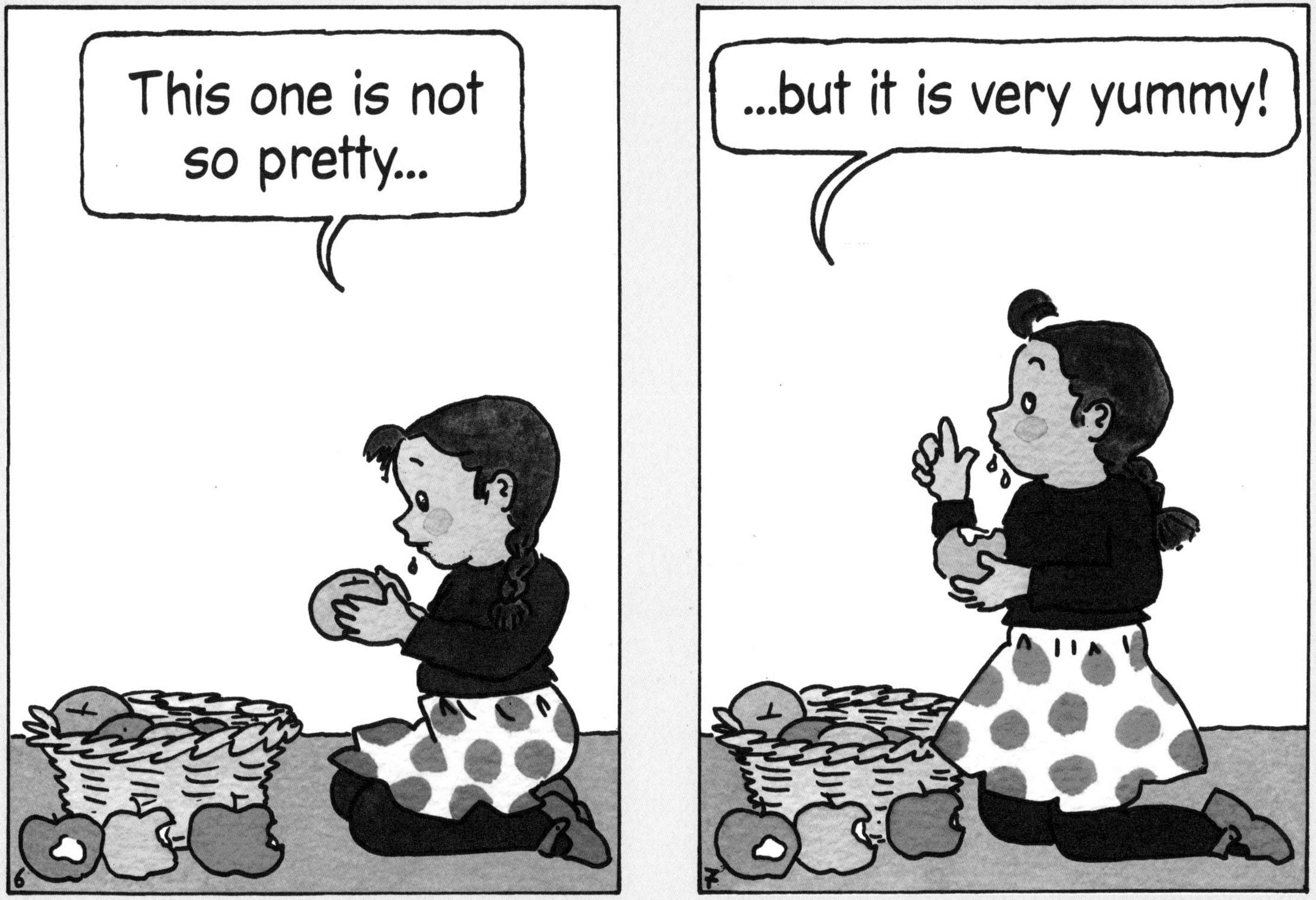
This one is not so pretty...
...but it is very yummy!

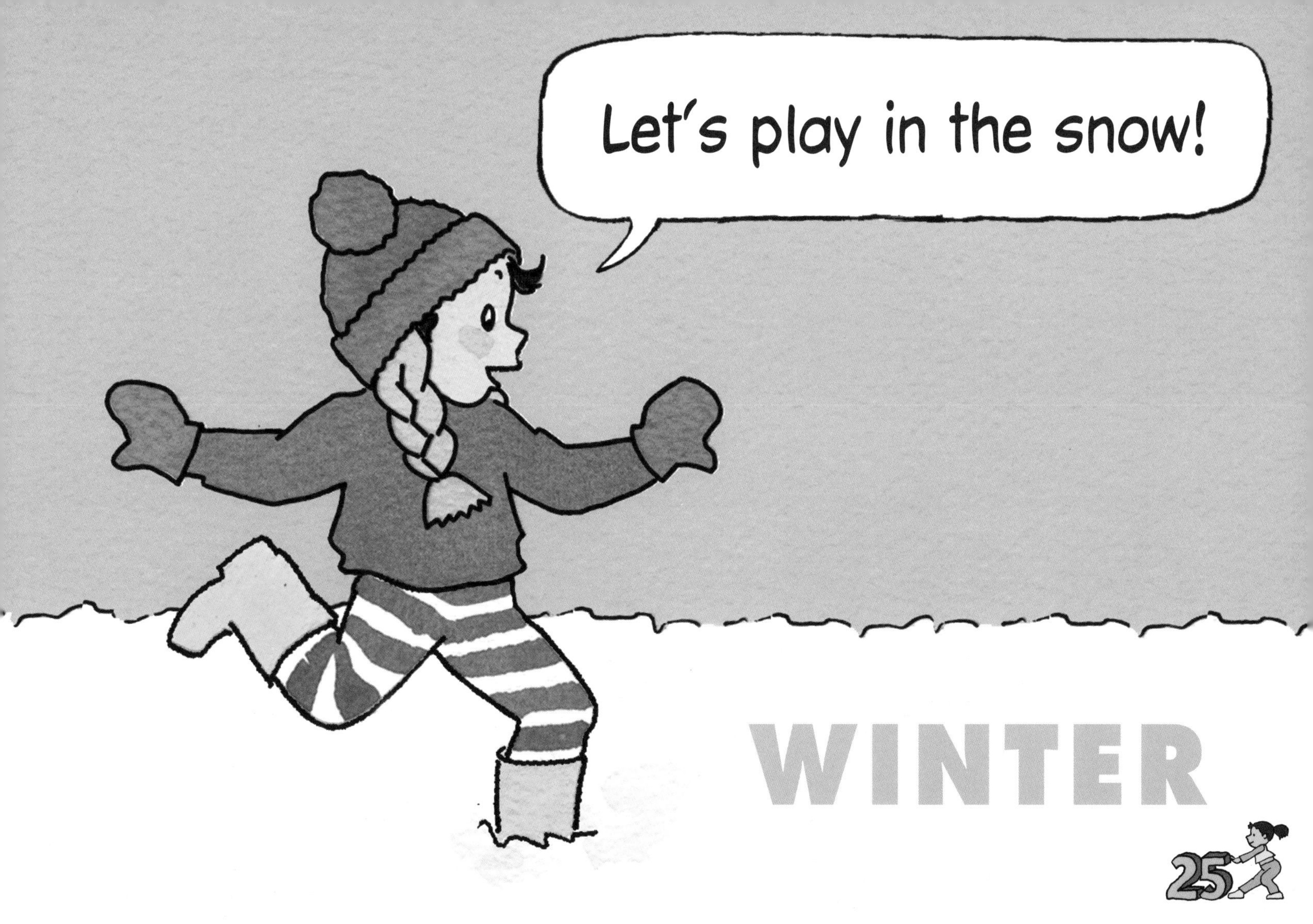
Let's play in the snow!
WINTER

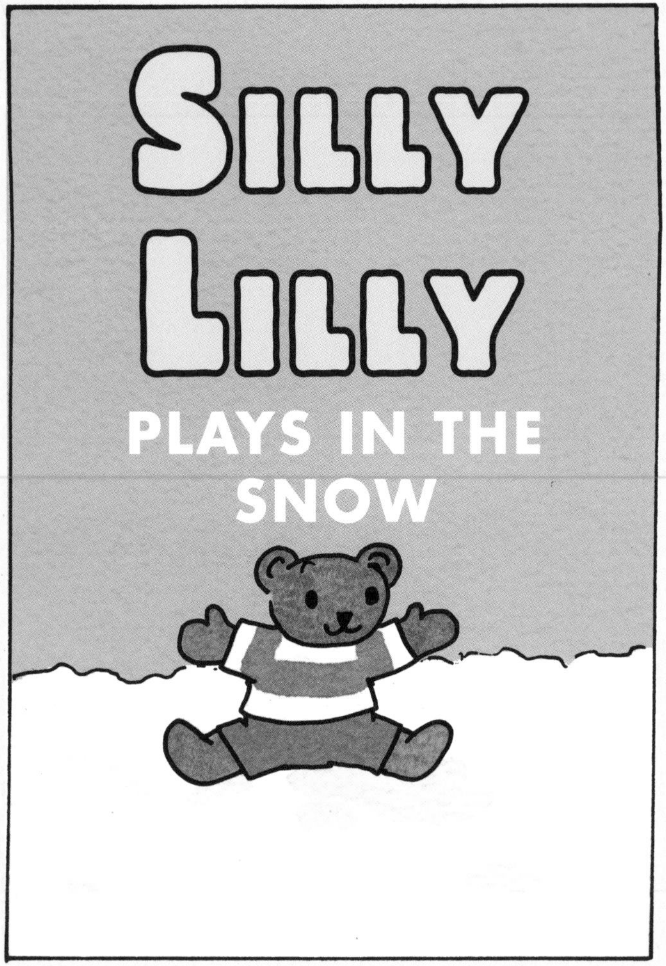
SILLY
LILLY
PLAYS IN THE
SNOW

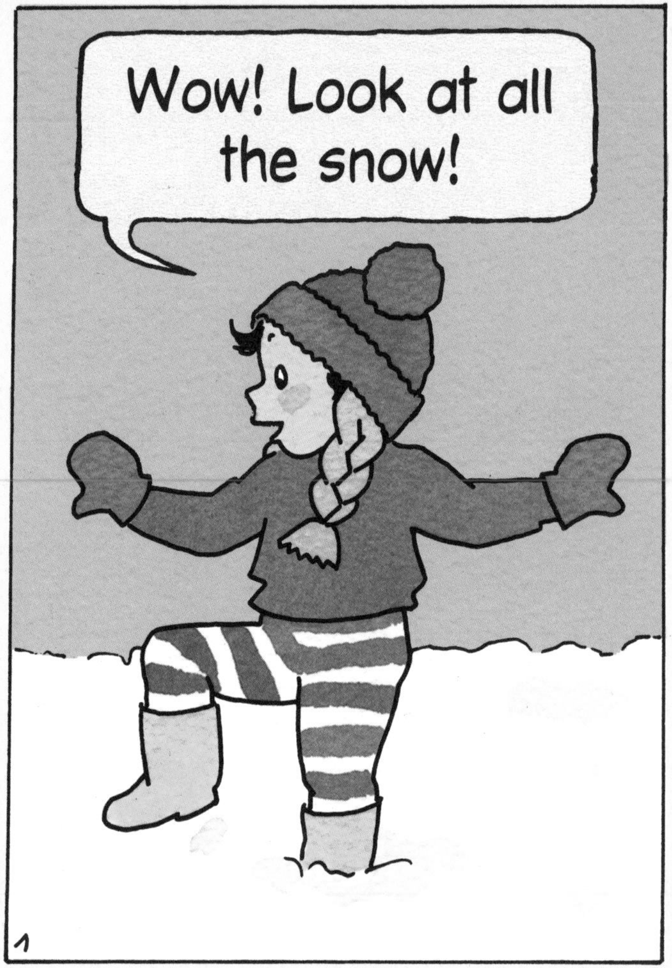
Wow! Look at all the snow!
1

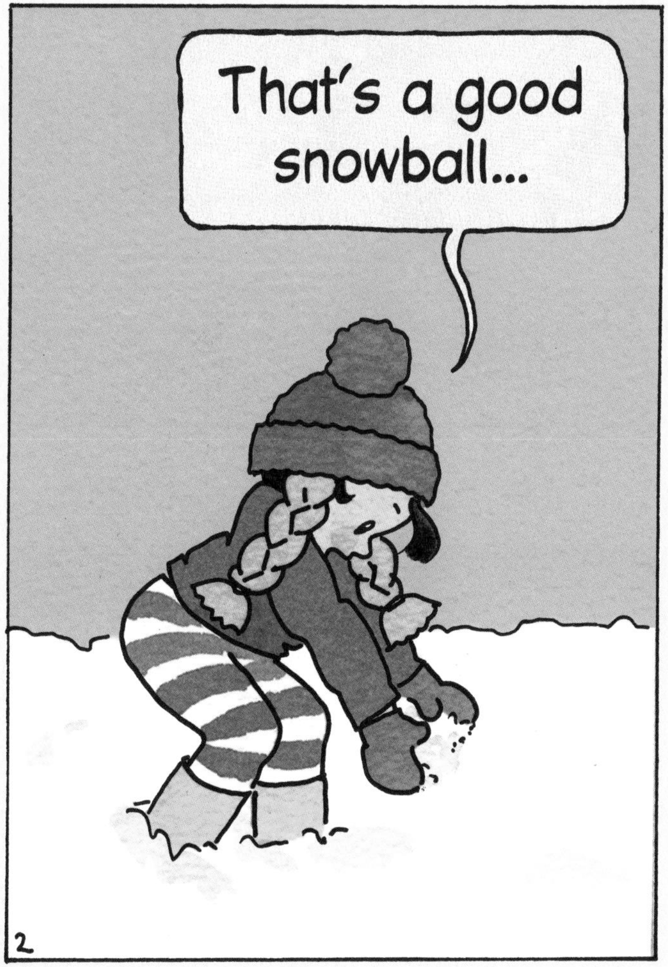
That's a good snowball...
2

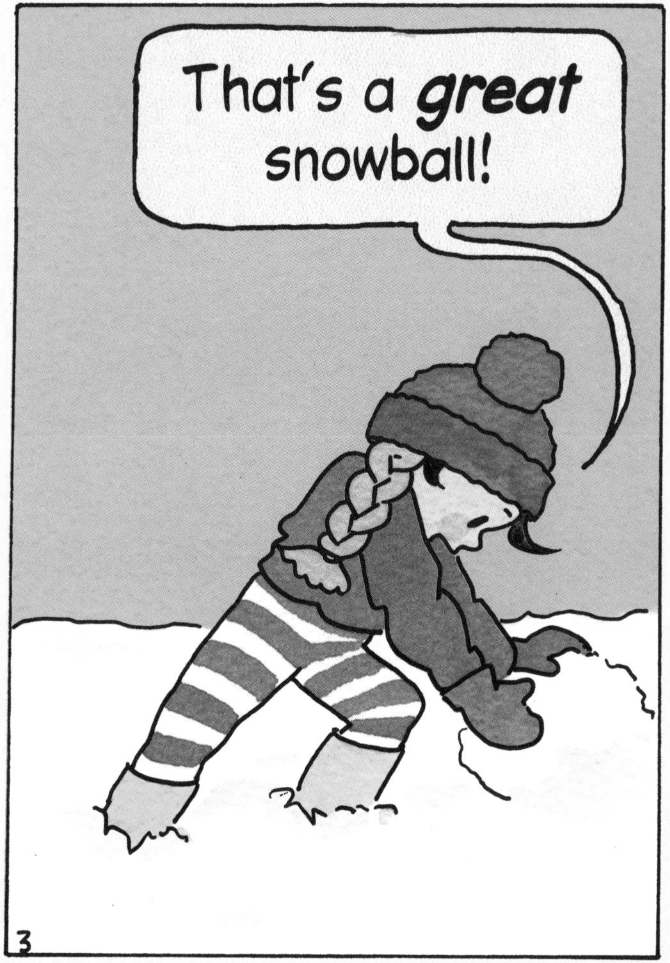
That's a great snowball!
3

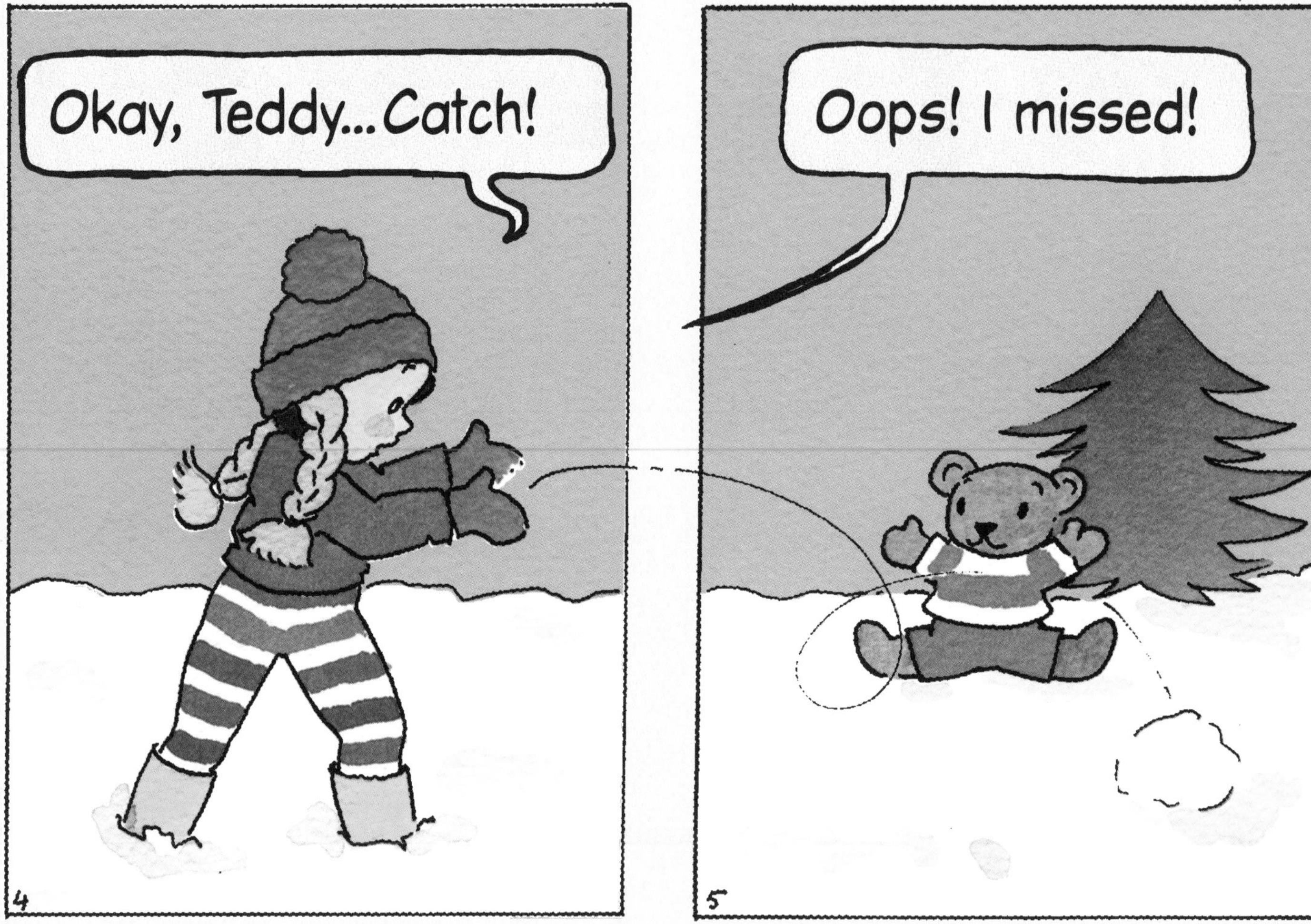
Okay, Teddy...Catch!
4
Oops! I missed!
5

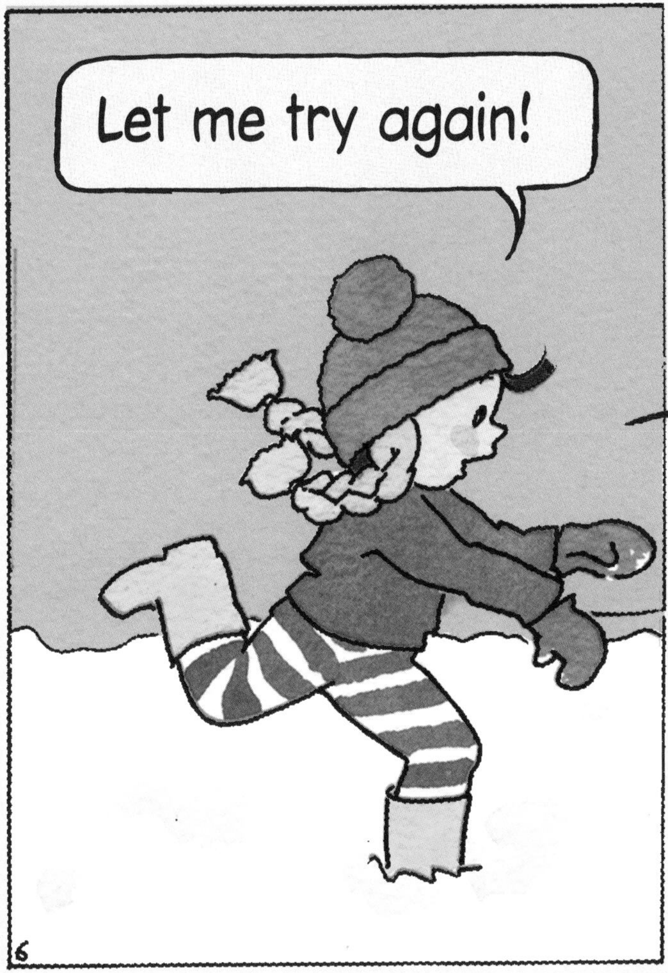
Let me try again!
6

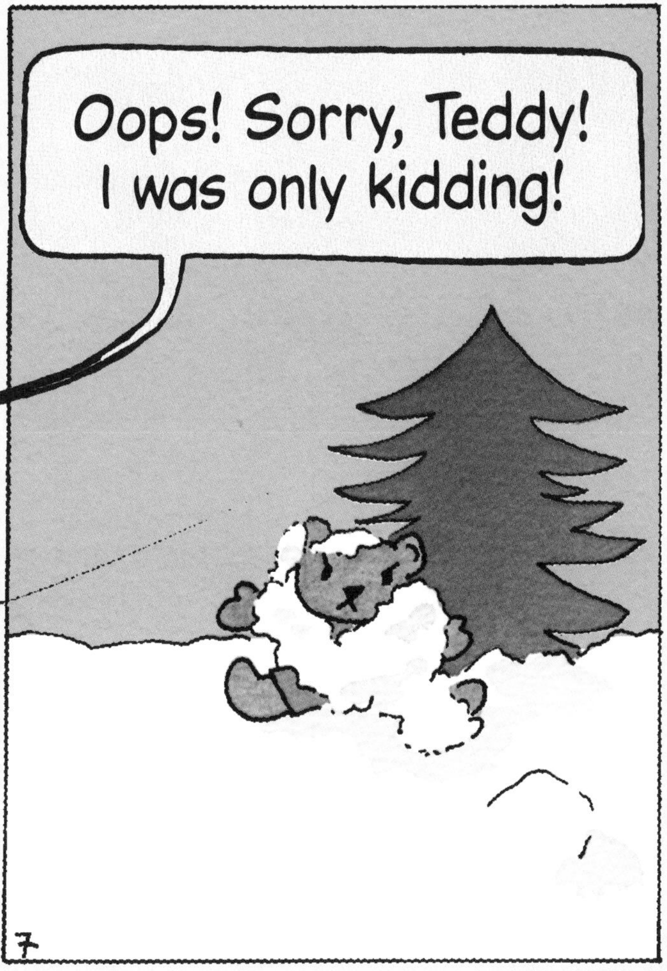
Oops! Sorry, Teddy! I was only kidding!
7

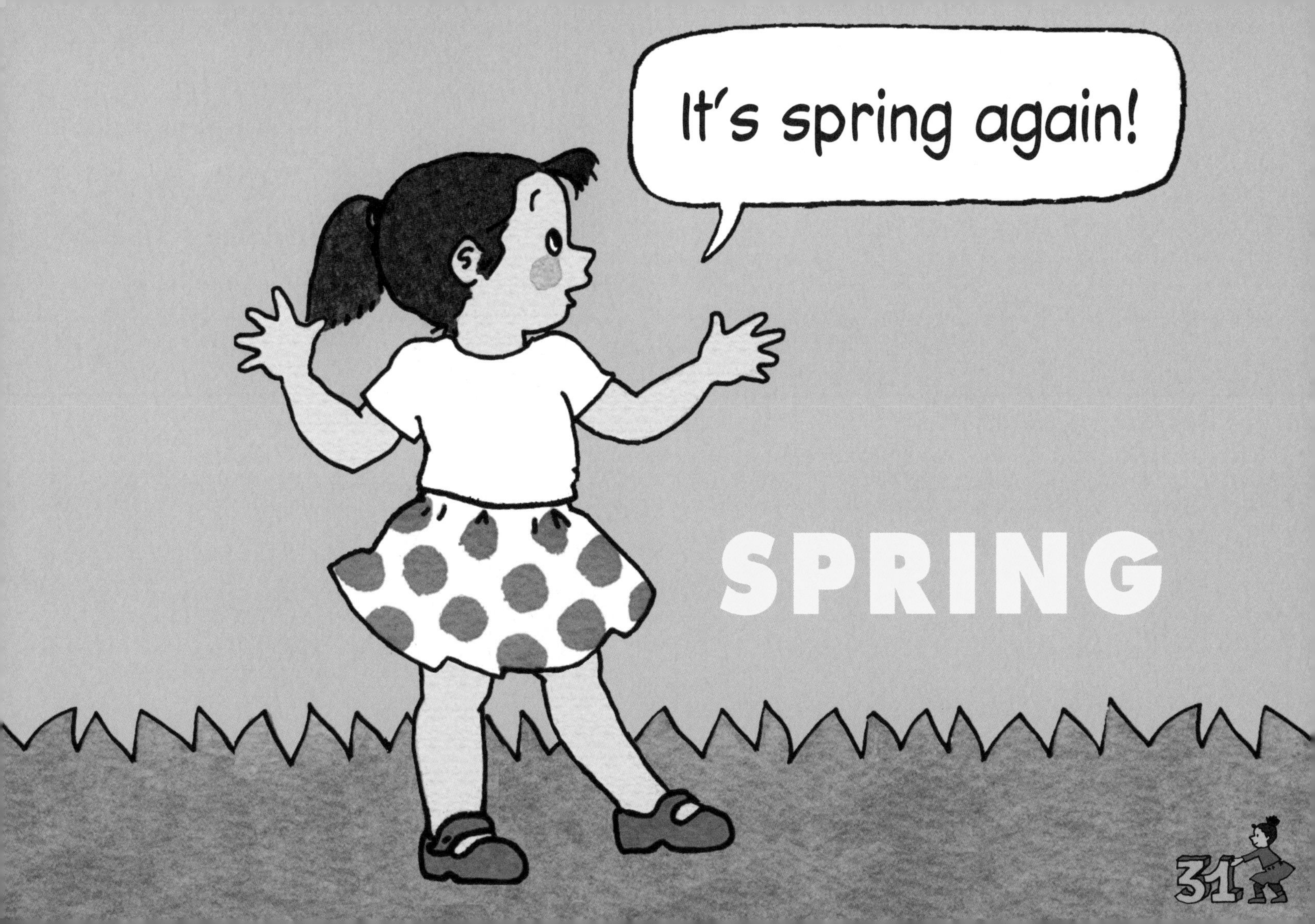
It's spring again!
SPRING

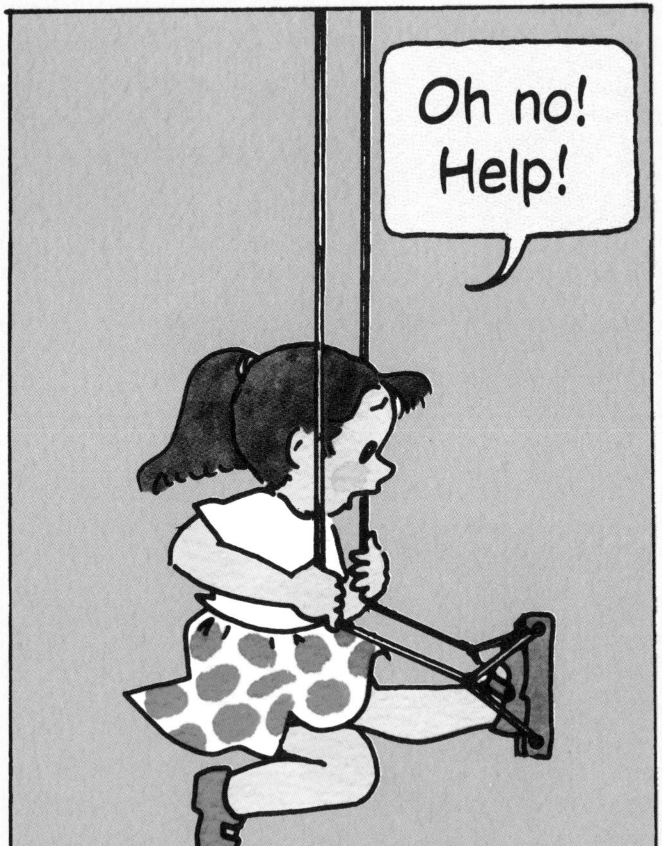
Oh no! Help!

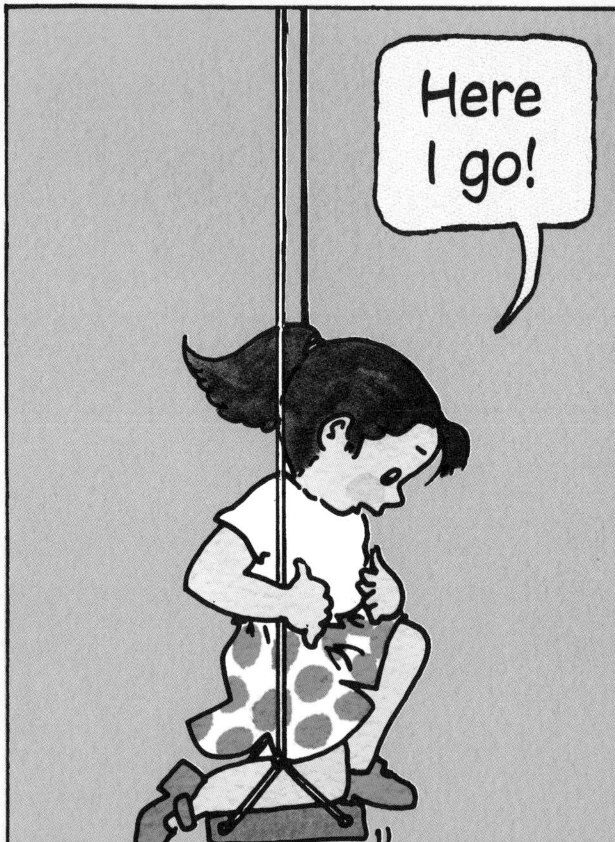
Here I go!

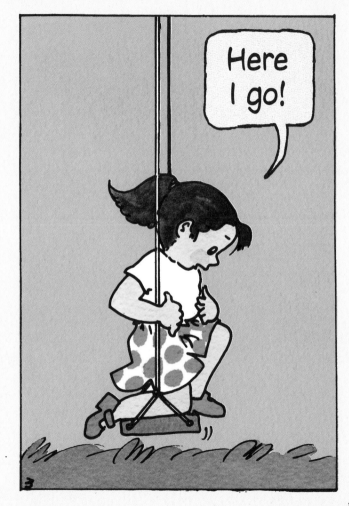

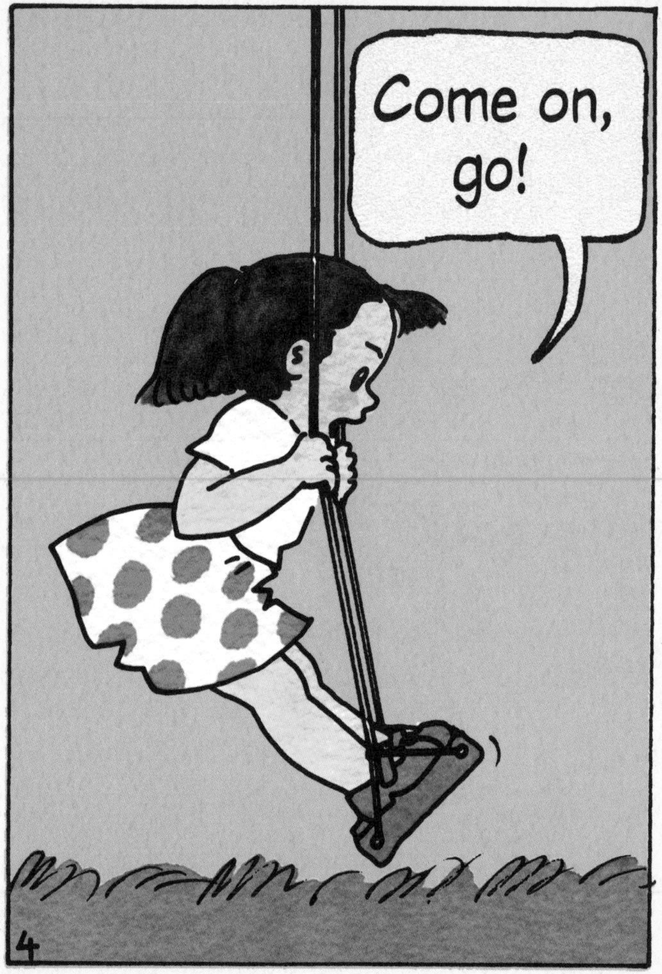
Come on, go!
4

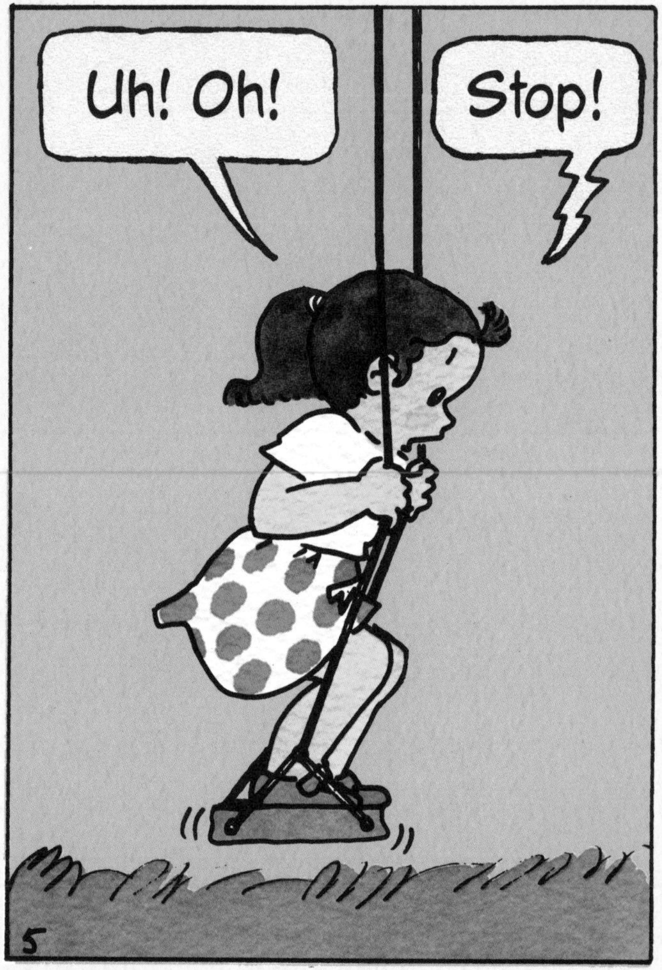
Uh! Oh!
Stop!
5

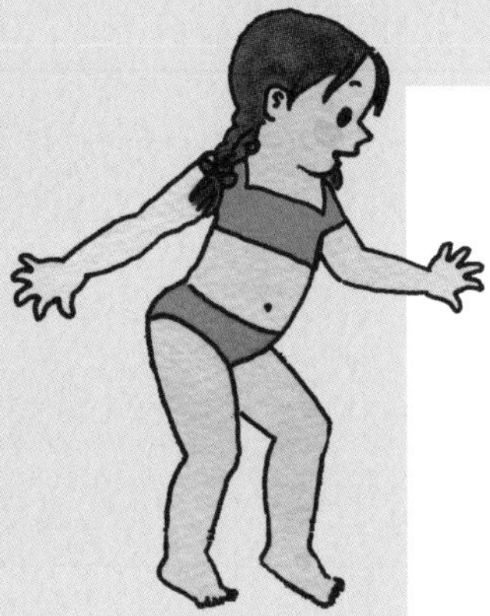

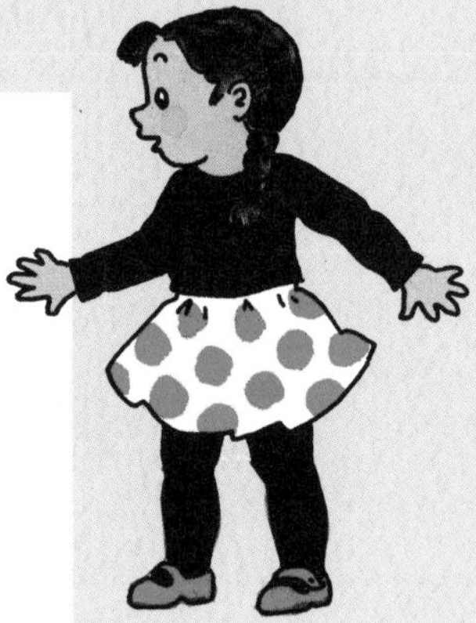

ABOUT THE AUTHOR

Agnès Rosenstiehl is the beloved writer and artist of nearly a hundred children's books, many featuring the deceptively simple antics of "Mimi Cracra," Silly Lilly's French alter ego. In 1995, she received the prestigious Grand Prize for Children's Books from the Société des Gens de Lettres. Agnès formally studied literature as well as music, and is married to an eminent mathematician. She lives in a country house with a garden, hidden in the center of Paris. She has four children and fifteen grandchildren.

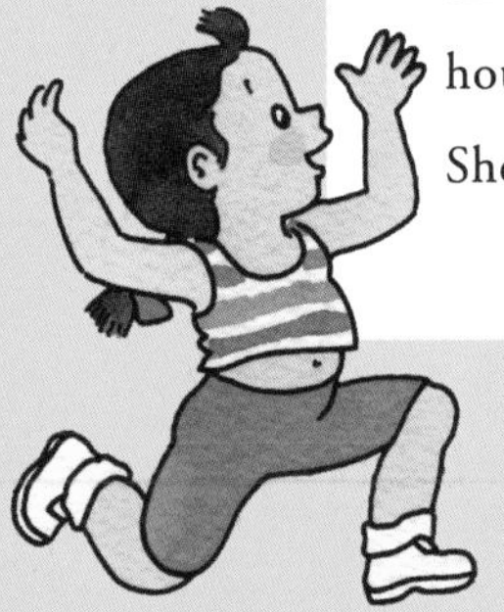

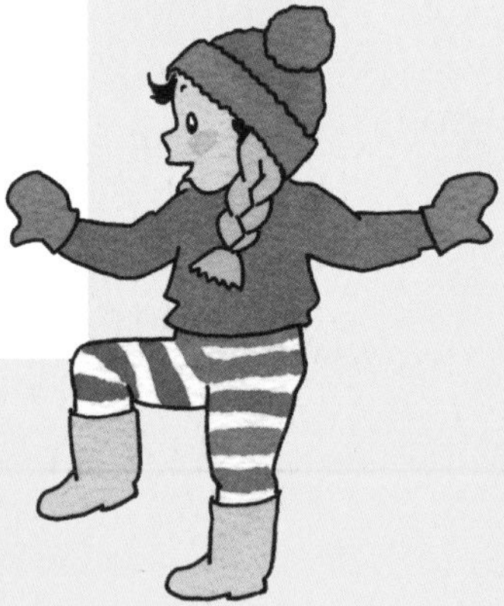

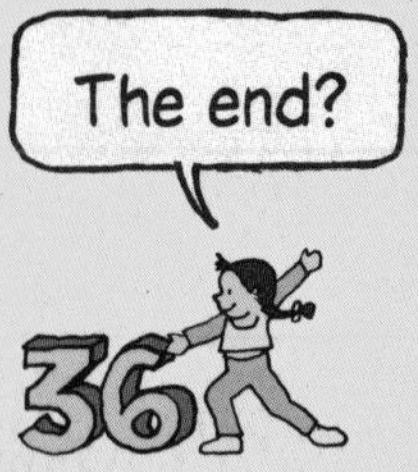
The end?